To Betsy Hass,
Daniel Ezra, Raphael, Abigail and Akira

VIKING
Published by the Penguin Group
Penguin Putnam Books for Young Readers, 345 Hudson Street, New York, New York 10014, U.S.A.
Penguin Books Ltd, 27 Wrights Lane, London W8 5TZ, England
Penguin Books Australia Ltd, Ringwood, Victoria, Australia
Penguin Books Canada Ltd, 10 Alcorn Avenue, Toronto, Ontario, Canada M4V 3B2
Penguin Books (N.Z.) Ltd, 182-190 Wairau Road, Auckland 10, New Zealand

Penguin Books Ltd, Registered Offices: Harmondsworth, Middlesex, England

First published in 1982 by The Viking Press. This edition published in 1999 by Viking,
a member of Penguin Putnam Books for Young Readers.

7 9 10 8

LIBRARY OF CONGRESS CATALOGING-IN-PUBLICATION DATA
Keats, Ezra Jack.
Clementina's cactus / Ezra Jack Keats.   p.   cm.
Summary: After a rainstorm, Clementina and her father discover a
surprise in the prickly skin of the cactus that they've watched growing in the desert.
ISBN 0-670-88545-2
[1.Cactus—Fiction. 2. Deserts—Fiction. 3. Stories without words.] I. Title.
PZ7.K2253C1 1999 [E]—dc21 98-47506 CIP AC

Manufactured in China

CLEMENTINA'S CACTUS

EZRA JACK KEATS

HOLP BOOK CO., LTD. TOKYO

VIKING

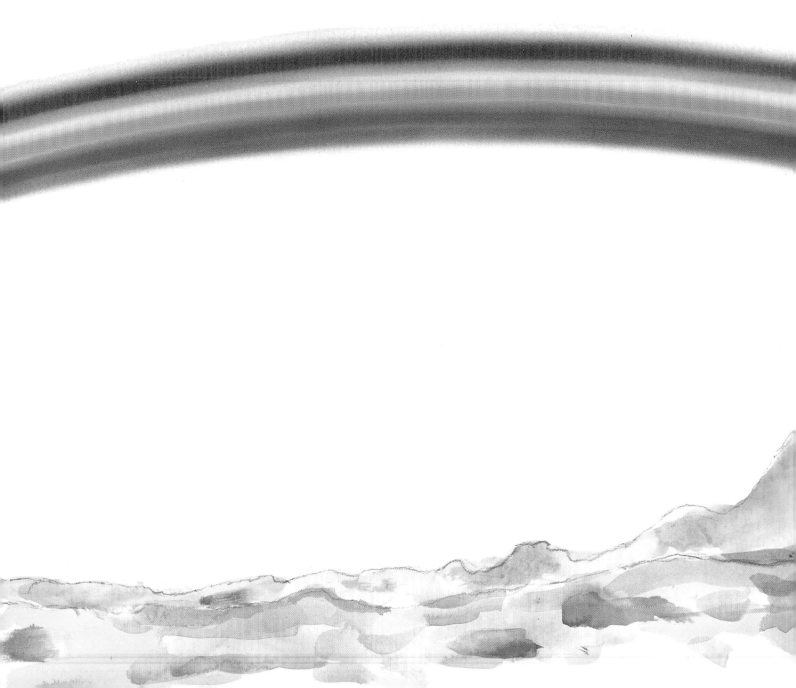